FUNNYBONES

FUNNYBONES

ALLAN AHLBERG · ANDRE AMSTUTZ

TED SMART

The Ghost Train

ALLAN AHLBERG · ANDRE AMSTUTZ

On a dark dark hill
there is a dark dark town.
In the dark dark town
there is a dark dark street.
Down the dark dark street
there is a dark dark station.
And in the dark dark station . . .

there is a ghost train!

Whooooooo!

One night, the big skeleton,
the little skeleton
and the dog skeleton
go for a ride on the ghost train.

They leave the dark dark cellar
and walk down the dark dark street.
They peep in at a few windows
on the way.

"How peaceful!" says the big skeleton.
"How nice!" the little skeleton says.

At the station
they get their tickets
from a monster
and have them punched
by another monster.
"How helpful!" says the big skeleton.
"How kind!" the little skeleton says.

At midnight, the ghost train arrives.
"Do you believe in ghosts?"
says the ghost.
"Yes!" the skeletons say.
"Good," says the ghost.
"Climb aboard!"

And off they go —
out of the dark dark station,
out of the dark dark town,
up and over the dark dark hill
and into the dark dark night.

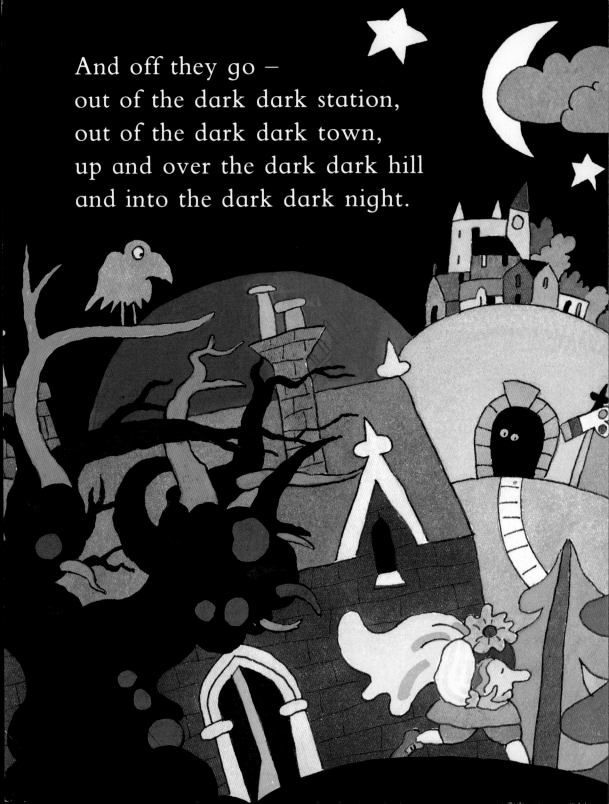

The three skeletons
sit next to a big monster
and share a joke
with a little monster.
"How friendly!" says the big skeleton.
"What fun!" the little skeleton says.

At one o'clock the train arrives
at Ghost-Town-by-the-Sea.

The skeletons leave the train
and stroll around.
They kick the ghost of a ball
and catch the ghost of a fish.
They paddle in the dark dark sea
and ride on the dark dark donkeys.

They watch
THE MONSTERS' BEAUTY PARADE.

"How charming!" says the big skeleton.
"What glamour!" the little skeleton says.

At three o'clock
the ghost train whistle blows.
It is time to leave.
The skeletons climb aboard
and off they go –
away from the dark dark sea,
away from the dark dark sand,
in and out of the very dark dark tunnel
and into the dark dark night.

At four o'clock
the train arrives at the station.

The big skeleton, the little skeleton
and the dog skeleton hurry home.
They peep in at a few windows
on the way.
Suddenly, a <u>baby</u> cries.
(Do you believe in babies?)
"Waaaaa!"

"How frightful!" says the big skeleton.
"How scary!" the little skeleton says.
"How—l!" howls the dog.

And off they run –
into the house,
down the stairs,
into the cellar
and <u>under</u> the bed.

On a dark dark hill
there is a dark dark town.
In the dark dark town
there is a dark dark street.
Down the dark dark street
there is a dark dark station.
And in the dark dark station
there is a ghost train.

Would you like a ride?

The End

Dinosaur Dreams

ALLAN AHLBERG · ANDRE AMSTUTZ

In a dark dark street
there is a tall tall house.
In the tall tall house
there is a deep deep cellar.
In the deep deep cellar
there is a cosy cosy bed.
And in the cosy cosy bed . . .

. . . three skeletons are dreaming.
The big skeleton is dreaming
about dinosaurs.
"I knew dinosaurs could run," he says
(in his dream).
"I never knew they had roller skates!"

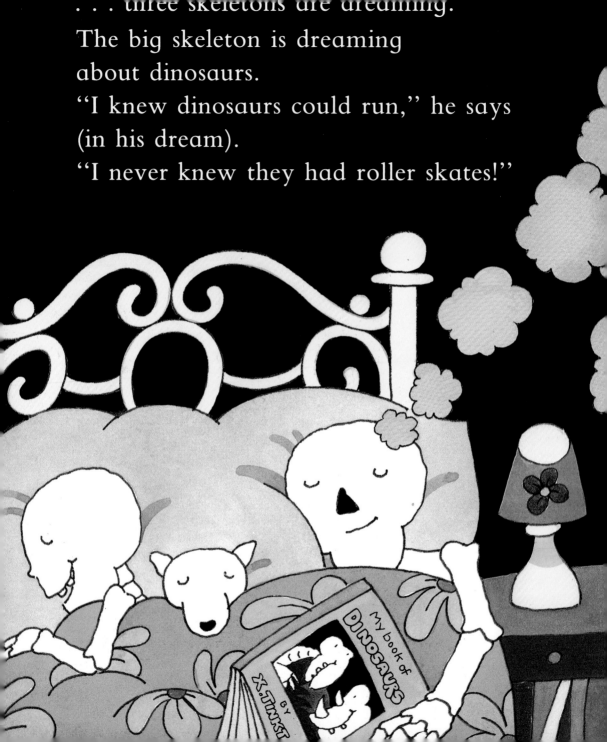

Suddenly, the big skeleton is chased
by a very big dinosaur.
"You can't scare me," he says.
"You're just a dream."
"Grr!" growls the dinosaur.
"Help!" shouts the big skeleton.
And he runs away.

The little skeleton is dreaming
about dinosaurs, too.
"I knew dinosaurs could swim," he says.
"I never knew they had arm-bands!"

Suddenly, the little skeleton is chased
by a little dinosaur.
"You can't scare me," he says.
"You're just a fossil."
"Grr!" growls the dinosaur.
"Help!" shouts the little skeleton.
And <u>he</u> runs away.

The dog skeleton is also dreaming
about dinosaurs.
Suddenly, into his dream
comes the little skeleton
chased by a little dinosaur,
and the big skeleton
chased by a big dinosaur.

The dog skeleton
barks at the dinosaurs:
"Woof!"
And <u>he</u> chases <u>them</u>!
"Hooray!" says the big skeleton.
"Hooray!" says the little skeleton.
"Give that dog a bone!"

The dinosaurs run away.

The dinosaurs swim away.

The dinosaurs fly away.

But the dog skeleton finds them
and chases them again.
The dinosaurs don't look
where they are going.
Suddenly, there is a great big crash
and a very great big . . .

For some reason
(remember, this is a dream),

the big skeleton
and the little skeleton

put the dinosaur bones
together again.

They make the biggest dinosaur
the world has ever seen . . .

. . . and <u>it</u> chases them!

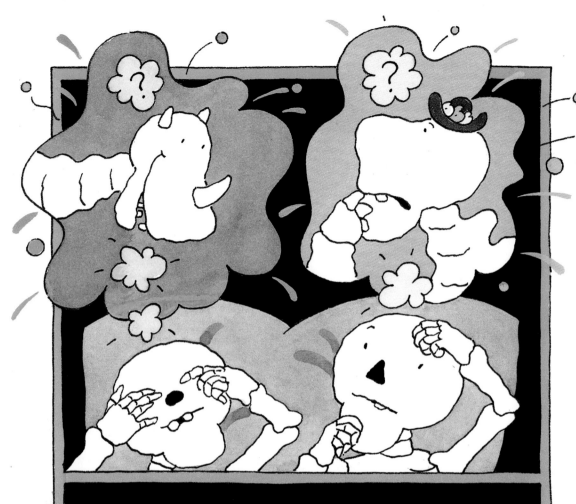

At last the big skeleton
and the little skeleton wake up.
They rub their eyes
and scratch their skulls.
They talk about their dreams.

"I had a dream about dinosaurs,"
says the big skeleton.
"You were in it."
"No, I wasn't," the little skeleton says.
"You were in mine!"

After that, the big skeleton says,
"What shall we do now?"
"Let's take the dog for a walk,"
says the little skeleton.
"Good idea!" the big skeleton says.

But the dog skeleton
isn't ready for a walk.
He is still sleeping.
He has a dream bone
in his dream mouth . . .

DOGOSAURUS REX

. . . and does not want to be disturbed.

The End

Mystery Tour

ALLAN AHLBERG · ANDRE AMSTUTZ

In a dark dark town,
down a dark dark street,
in a dark dark car,
at a red red traffic light

. . . three skeletons are waiting.

"What shall we do tonight?"
says the big skeleton.
"Let's go on a mystery tour,"
the little skeleton says.
"Good idea!" says the big skeleton.
"What's a mystery tour?"
"I can't tell you,"
the little skeleton says.
"It's a mystery!"

Then the red red traffic light
turns green
. . . and the mystery tour begins.

The dark dark car drives
down the dark dark street
to mystery number one.

"What's that?" says the little skeleton.
"I know," the big skeleton says,
"it's a . . .

The dark dark car drives
down the dark dark street,
round the dark dark corner
to mystery number two.

"What's that?" says the big skeleton.
"I know," the little skeleton says,
"it's a . . .

. . . teddy in a tent!"

Two mysteries:
a teddy in a tent
and a baby in a cot.

The dark dark car drives
down the dark dark street,
past the dark dark park
and the dark dark zoo
to mystery number three.

"I know," says the big skeleton,
"it's a . . .

NUMBER 3

. . . black cat on a roof!"

And mystery number four.
"It's a bag of bones,"
the little skeleton says.
"No, it's not," says the big skeleton.
"If we put them all together, it's a . . .

"Whoooooo!" goes mystery number five.
And what is it. . . ?

. . . A ghost on a train!

Five mysteries:
a ghost on a train,
a bag of bones
(that was really a parrot),
a black cat on a roof,
a teddy in a tent
and a baby in a cot.

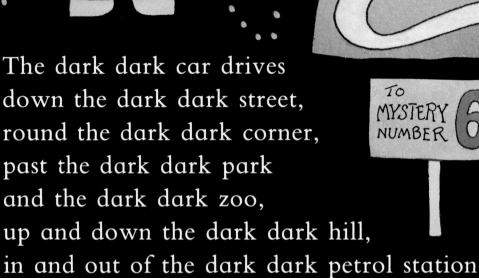

The dark dark car drives
down the dark dark street,
round the dark dark corner,
past the dark dark park
and the dark dark zoo,
up and down the dark dark hill,
in and out of the dark dark petrol station
to mystery number six.

TO
MYSTERY
NUMBER 6

"I know what mystery number six is," says the little skeleton.
"Me, too!" the big skeleton says, "it's . . .

Now the mystery tour is ended . . .
well, nearly.
There's just one more mystery.
"What's that?" says the little skeleton.
"Where's the car?"
the big skeleton says.

A dark dark car
in a dark dark car-park
is hard to find.

The End

Skeleton Crew

ALLAN AHLBERG · ANDRE AMSTUTZ

On a dark dark night,
on a dark dark sea,
in a dark dark boat
three skeletons float . . .

on a holiday.

The big one is dozing
in his deck chair.
"Zzz!"

The dog one is dozing
in his hammock.
"Zzz!"
The little one is fishing.

I've got a bite!

The little skeleton
catches a fish
and throws it back.

He catches a boot
and throws it back.

He catches an octopus . . . .

The big skeleton catches a little fish
and throws it back.
He catches a big fish and keeps it.
He catches a bigger fish . . .

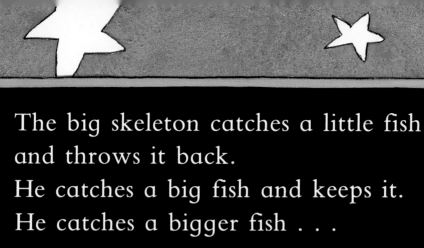

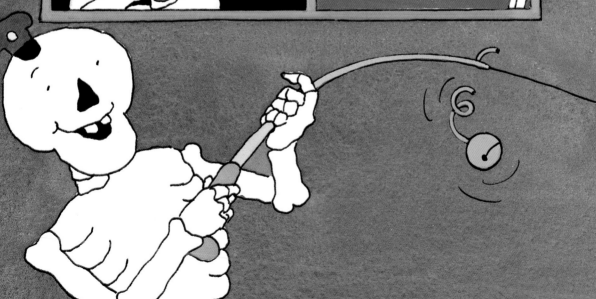

And – "Yo – ho – ho!" –
the <u>pirates</u> come.

The pirates climb aboard
looking for treasure.
They steal the deck chair
and the hammock.

They steal the fishing rod
and the cat fish.
"Miaow!"
They steal . . . the boat!

The next night . . .
nothing happens.

But the <u>next</u> night,
under a starry sky
and over the deep blue sea,
the skeletons spy . . . a tree.
"Yippee!"

On the island
the big skeleton
finds a parrot.
"Pretty Polly!"

The little one finds a coconut.
"Clonk!"
And the dog finds a crab.

Also, somebody finds them.

The next night a lot happens.
A storm blows up.
The thunder crashes,
the lightning flashes,
the wind howls
and the dog howls, too.
"Howl!"

As quick as a blink
the raft is blown
across the foam . . .

The End (or is it?)

The End

The Pet Shop

ALLAN AHLBERG · ANDRE AMSTUTZ

In a dark dark – Woof! – street
there is a dark dark – Woof! – house.
Behind the dark dark – Woof! – house
there is a dark dark – Woof! – garden.
In the dark dark – Woof! – garden
there is a very dark dark –
Woof! – hole

... and a little noisy dog – Woof!

One night, the big skeleton
and the little skeleton
go into the garden.
"I'm fed up with this dog,"
says the little skeleton.
"Me, too," says the big skeleton.
"All he does is dig holes – and bark."
"Woof!" barks the dog.

"I know," says the little skeleton,
"let's go to the pet shop —
    and swop him."
"Good idea!" the big skeleton says.
"Howl!" howls the dog.

So off they – Woof! – go,
out of the dark dark garden,
down the dark dark street
and into the dark dark – Miaow! –
– Squeak! – Grunt! – pet shop.
The big skeleton and the little skeleton
swop the dog – Woof! – skeleton

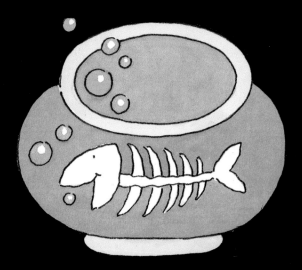

. . . for a goldfish.

But after a night or two . . .
"I'm fed up with this goldfish,"
says the little skeleton.

"Me, too," says the big skeleton.
"All it does is blow bubbles —
and swim."

So off they go again,
out of the dark dark house,
down the dark dark street
and back to the dark dark – Miaow! –
– Snort! – Croak! – pet shop.
The big skeleton and the little skeleton
swop the goldfish – Bubble, bubble! – skeleton
. . . for a parrot.

SHORTY!

But after another night or two . . .
"I'm fed up with this parrot,"
says the little skeleton.
"Me, too," says the big skeleton.
"All he does is shout rude names."
"Big bum!" shouts the parrot.

Big Bum!

I'm fed up

. . . for a hippopotamus.
But the hippopotamus
is no good either.
All he does . . .

. . . is fill the room!

And after a night or two . . .
"I love this rabbit,"
says the little skeleton.
"Me, too," says the big skeleton.
"He's not big,
he's not cheeky
and he doesn't blow bubbles."

The only trouble is — <u>he</u> is not a <u>he</u>.

So after a few more nights . . .
"I'm fed up with these rabbits,"
says the little skeleton.
"And these!" the big skeleton says.

Back they go to the pet shop.
"And I'm fed up with this
– Miaow! – Moo! – Baa! –
pet shop as well!"
says the little skeleton.

The pet shop skeleton
puts the rabbits in a hutch.
"Cheer up!" he says.
"I've got just the thing for you."

He gives them a big box
with little holes in it.
"But don't open it until
you get home."

After that the big skeleton
and the little skeleton
leave the dark dark –
Miaow! – pet shop, and
hurry down the dark dark street
to the dark dark house
. . . and the dark dark cellar.

They put the box on the table.
"I wonder what it is,"
says the little skeleton.
"Me, too," says the big skeleton.
. . . "WOOF!" barks the box.

The End

The Black Cat

ALLAN AHLBERG · ANDRE AMSTUTZ

In a dark dark town,
on a cold cold night,
under a starry starry sky,
down a slippery slippery slope,
on a bumpety bumpety sledge . . .

a little skeleton is sliding . . .
and sliding . . .
and crashing – wallop!

The little skeleton
loses a leg in the snow.
A white leg in snow
is hard to find.
A black cat in snow
is easy to find.
What is <u>she</u> doing here?

The little skeleton and the big skeleton
go to the bone-yard
to get a new leg
for the little skeleton.

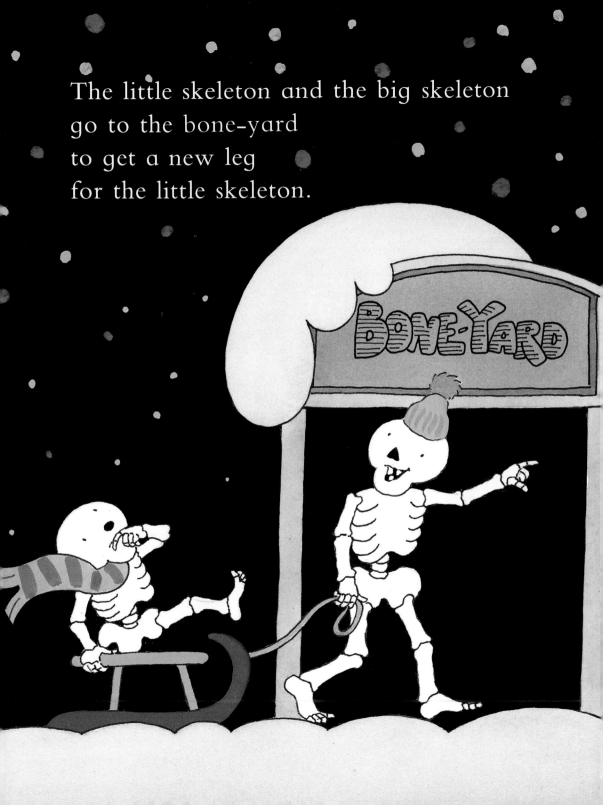

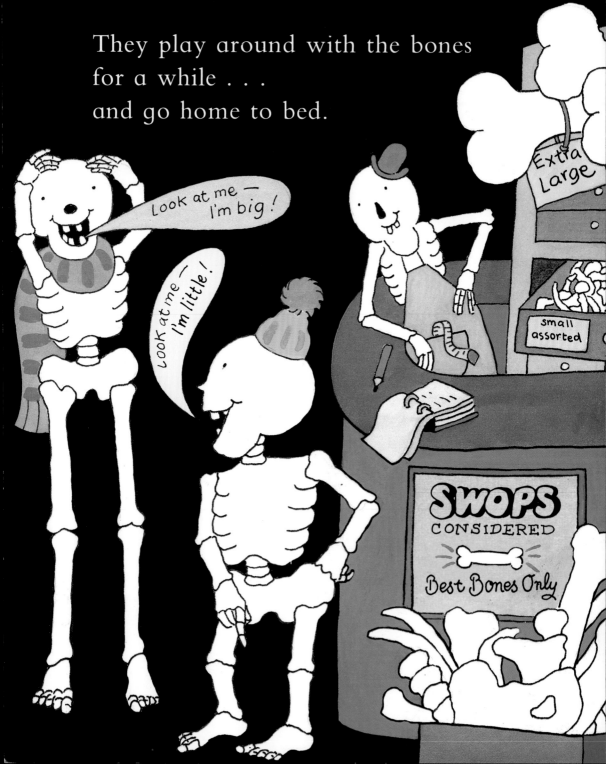

Then . . .
in the dark dark town,
on <u>another</u> cold cold night,
under a starry starry sky,
down a slippery slippery slope,
on a bumpety bumpety sledge. . . .

CRASH

<u>two</u> skeletons are sliding . . .
and sliding . . .
and sliding . . .
and crashing – bang!
WALLOP!
This time the big skeleton
loses a leg in the snow.

A white leg in snow
is hard to find.
A black cat is easy.
Is she still here?
I wonder why.

The big skeleton
and the little skeleton
go to the bone-yard
to get a new leg
for the big skeleton.

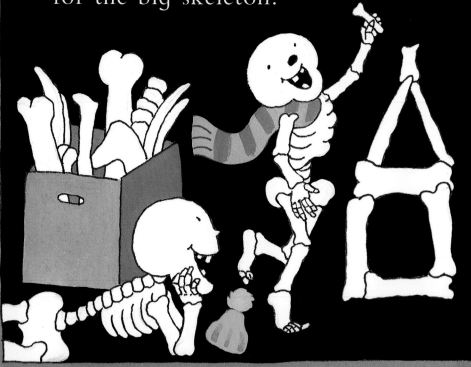

They play around again with the bones
and go home to bed.

Then . . .
in the dark town,
on the <u>next</u> night,
under a starry sky,
with a moon, too,
down a slippery slope,
in the frosty air,
on a bumpety sledge . . .

three skeletons are sliding . . .
and sliding . . .
and shouting . . .
and barking!
And banging! Wallop!

CRASH!

This time the big skeleton
and the little skeleton
lose the dog skeleton.
A white dog in snow
is hard to find.
But a noisy dog is easy to find.
So is a black cat!

The dog skeleton chases the cat.
Now we know –
<u>that's</u> what she is here for!

The dog chases the cat
up and down
the dark dark hill,
in and out
of the dark dark bone-yard,

round and round
the dark dark streets
and down and down
to the dark dark cellar.

But a black cat in a cellar
is very hard to find.
Can <u>you</u> see her?

Well, the dog skeleton couldn't,
and the little skeleton couldn't,
and the big skeleton didn't even try.
So off they went – at last – to bed.

Meanwhile . . .
in the same town,
on the same night,
under the same sky,
down the same slope,
a bumpety sledge is sliding . . .

with a black cat on it.

This edition published in 1995
for The Book People, Guardian House,
Borough Road, Godalming, Surrey GU7 2AE
by William Heinemann Ltd
an imprint of Reed Books Ltd
Michelin House, 81 Fulham Road, London SW3 6RB
and Auckland, Melbourne, Singapore and Toronto

The Pet Shop and The Black Cat first published 1990
by William Heinemann Ltd
Text copyright © Allan Ahlberg 1990
Illustrations copyright © André Amstutz 1990

Dinosaur Dreams and Mystery Tour first published 1991
by William Heinemann Ltd
Text copyright © Allan Ahlberg 1991
Illustrations copyright © André Amstutz 1991

Skeleton Crew and The Ghost Train first published 1992
by William Heinemann Ltd
Text copyright © Allan Ahlberg 1991
Illustrations copyright © André Amstutz 1991

ISBN 1-85613-247-1
Produced by Mandarin Offset Ltd
Printed and bound in Hong Kong